STEALING THE SHOW

BY PERDITA FINN

SCHOLASTIC INC.
New York   Toronto   London   Auckland   Sydney
Mexico City   New Delhi   Hong Kong   Buenos Aires

For Sophie and Jonah
Who Never Get to Go Anywhere

ISBN 0-439-74433-4

Text copyright © 2006 by Perdita Finn
Illustrations copyright © 2006 by Scholastic Inc.

12 11 10 9 8 7 6 5 4 3 2 1   6 7 8 9 10 11/0

Printed in the U.S.A.
First printing, March 2006

Cover and chapter opener illustration by Brandon Dorman
Additional illustrations by Mike Moran

1 ENTER STRANGER

"Oh, Romeo, Romeo!" said Josh in a high-pitched voice.

"Take a chill pill, Josh!" snapped Katie. "I told you, I don't want to be Juliet. I want a part where I get to sword fight."

"Good. 'Cause you're too much of a toad to be Juliet."

After dinner Katie had been practicing lines for the middle school play. Josh, her older brother, was supposed to be finishing his math homework but really was playing with his Game Boy under the dining room table — and making fun of his sister.

Katie picked up her pencil and threw it at him.

"Cut it out!" Josh shouted as the pencil whizzed by his ear.

"Josh, do your homework!" called Mr. Lexington, who was washing dishes at the sink.

Josh was making a spitball to hurl at Katie, and she was trying to kick his leg, when they heard a knock.

Later Katie said she'd seen a flash of blue light. And Josh said he'd heard a faraway sonic boom. But it was the knock that made them stop fighting.

"Can one of you kids get that?" said their father, wiping his sudsy hands on a dish towel.

"Now, who could it be at this time of night?" muttered Mrs. Lexington. She put down her scissors and the scrapbook she always started for the children at the beginning of the school year and began straightening pillows on the couch.

Josh leaped up and raced to the front door. But Katie slid across the hardwood floor and managed to squeeze in front of him, grabbing the handle first. They ended up opening the door together.

Standing on their front porch in the darkness was a boy no taller than Josh.

But he didn't look like a kid from the neighborhood.

With the light spilling out from the hallway, Josh and Katie could see he was wearing a flat, black hat squashed on his head. He had long, dirty-blond hair down to his shoulders. He was wearing a cape and what looked like puffy shorts, and tights that were covered in stains and patches.

And he smelled.

As soon as they opened the door, it hit their noses. It was the smell of smoke and sweat and unwashed bathrooms and cooking onions all mixed up together. It was strong. At the same instant, Josh and Katie looked at each other, wondering who this kid was.

"Halloween isn't until the end of next month," said Josh. Katie nodded her head.

"Greetings, my friends. I apologize for the lateness of the hour. I know 'tis near the second watch, but Master Dee insisted I must come now."

"Dee? Dee?" Josh and Katie's mother rushed forward, a worried expression on her face. "Not *Mr.* Dee who runs the exchange program? Why, I haven't heard from him in months!"

"Ah, lady! Thou must be Mistress Lexington!" The blond boy took off his hat and made a sweeping bow.

A smile instantly spread across Mrs. Lexington's plump, round face. She blushed and patted her curly black hair into place.

"Oh, hello," she answered and did a little bow back. Katie groaned. Her mother was always imitating people she'd just met.

"Come in. Come in. Please do," Mrs. Lexington said. She pushed Josh and Katie out of the way and took the boy by the arm. Josh could see her nose wrinkle from the smell.

Mr. Lexington, his apron still on, appeared in the hall. "Is this a friend of yours?" he whispered to the kids. They both shook their heads, then followed Mrs. Lexington into the living room.

"Good friends, I am Jack Bradford," the boy announced. He bowed again, unbuckled a long belt with a sword attached, and tossed it onto one of the armchairs.

"Cool!" said Josh, at the sight of its shining blade. "Is that real?"

"Aye. What knew I of the perils I should meet in such new worlds?"

"Ah . . . Jack," chimed in Mrs. Lexington, hovering by the chair. "You must be our exchange student."

"What?" gasped Josh and Katie at the same time. But Mrs. Lexington shushed them before they could say anything else.

"Yes, madam. I trust you were prepared for my arrival?"

"Well, not really, dear. But we're so happy you're here. That's the important thing. These are my children, Joshua and Katie, and my husband, Abner Lexington."

Mr. Lexington had been taking off his glasses and polishing them on his shirt, then putting them on and taking them off again as if he couldn't see. He looked up when he was introduced. "Ah, hi, Jack," he said. "You know my wife from the real estate office?"

Mrs. Lexington glared at her husband. "Abner, weren't you listening? Jack is our foreign exchange student. He's going to be living with us."

Jack nodded his head. "Parchments, madam," he said, pulling some musty-looking documents out of a bag strapped around his waist and handing them to Mrs. Lexington. "Master Dee requested I give them to you."

"Oh, yes . . . yes, everything's here," said Mrs. Lexington, glancing at the papers while Josh and Katie peered over her shoulder. "Well, Jack, I guess you're with us for a month. Isn't that terrific, kids?" Josh and Katie looked at each other and then at the strange boy who was moving into their house. Terrific?

"Terrific, terrific," echoed Mr. Lexington absent-mindedly. "Well, I guess I better get back to those dishes. I think I must have left something burning on the stove. Whew! What a smell!" He started to head out of the room, but Mrs. Lexington grabbed him by the arm.

"You stay here and get to know Jack, Abner. Now, can I get you anything to eat, dear?"

"Aye!" said Jack, heartily. "Have you cakes and ale?"

"Ale? You mean *beer*?" said Mrs. Lexington, her eyes wide.

"Aye. Or if not ale, then wine shall do. I've a powerful thirst."

Josh and Katie looked at each other. Who *was* this kid? And was he really going to be living with them?

Mrs. Lexington gave a nervous little laugh. "I know you have a different drinking age in Europe, but here in America . . ."

"Am I really in the New World, then?" gasped Jack, looking around him.

"Now, Jack," continued Mrs. Lexington, "I'm happy to welcome you into our family, but we will expect you to follow the same rules as our own children, and there will certainly be no under-age drinking in this house."

"How about some juice and a sandwich, Jack?" offered Mr. Lexington.

"Juice? Sandwich?" Jack said the words as if he'd never heard them before.

Mrs. Lexington smiled, nodded her head, and went to the kitchen.

"You're a lucky kid, Jack," said Mr. Lexington. "My wife, Betsy, makes the best PB and J you ever tasted. Right, kids?"

But neither Josh nor Katie answered.

Josh was still checking out the sword. Carefully, he touched the rough, leather-covered handle and then put his finger on the blade. It was sharp. Really sharp.

Katie was watching Jack. Something wasn't right and she knew it. He was walking around the living room peering at the wallpaper, the glass on the windows, the books. He kept touching things as if they were made of some alien material. "S'blood!" he whispered under his breath.

"What did you say?" Katie asked suspiciously.

"My lady," he said and bowed to her.

8

"What?" said Katie.

"What?" said Josh. "She's no lady, Jack. Believe me. She's a toad. A total toad."

"Shut your face, Josh!"

"Kids, kids," interrupted their father. "Remember, we've got a guest."

"Sir," said Jack, turning to Mr. Lexington. "Thou dost me great honor to take me into thine palace." Josh and Katie looked around the room. They loved their house, but it wasn't a palace, just a split-level ranch like all the others on the block. "I may be of humble birth, sir," Jack continued, "but I promise I shall not dishonor you."

Josh tried to stifle a laugh. "What grade are you in, anyway?" he asked.

But before Jack could answer, Mrs. Lexington returned with some food and set it down on the coffee table.

"Eat up, dear. You must be famished. We've heard how terrible that airplane food is."

Jack sipped the juice suspiciously. Then a smile broke out on his face. "Ah, sweet nectar of the gods. What call you this? *Juice?*"

"Yes, orange juice. I suppose you only get frozen in . . . in . . . Where *are* you from, dear?"

"The land of good Queen Bess, m'lady — England."

"Ah, England!" said Mr. Lexington, clearly pleased. "Now, Jack, I've got a couple of English stamps in my collection you might want to see. I may not have traveled far beyond Middlestock, but my stamps sure have. Mind if I show them to you later?"

"I would be honored, sir," said Jack. While Jack gulped down his food, letting the crumbs fall all over the carpet, Mr. Lexington began talking about a new stamp he'd been wanting to get from Australia. Jack gave a big yawn.

"You'll have to forgive Abner — he loves stamps." Mrs. Lexington smiled lovingly at her husband and stood up. "C'mon, Jack. We know you must be tired. We'll get everything straightened out in the morning. You'll share a room with my son, Joshua."

Josh threw a terrified look at his mother and held his nose behind Jack's back.

"And how about a bath before bed?" Mrs. Lexington added.

"Zounds, madam! My own dear sister took a bath and did die of the fever. God bless her sweet memory."

"Oh, I see. An early childhood trauma. . . ." murmured Mrs. Lexington. "Perhaps a shower, then," she announced brightly and, wrapping an arm around Jack Bradford, she guided him up the stairs.

2 BEHIND THE SCENES

"I can't believe Mom is going to let this stinky kid with a weapon stay in my room. What is going on? Has she totally flipped?"

"That's the question, isn't it? What is going on?"

Josh and Katie were still in the living room. Their father had gone back to the kitchen, and upstairs they could hear the sound of running water and muffled screams.

"Why is Mom always doing stuff like this?" asked Josh. "Remember the time she let the Lubkas leave Frank here for the weekend? He spent half the time trying to lock me in the closet and the other half eating everything in the refrigerator.

Ahhh! I can't take that again!" Josh threw himself down on the couch and started hitting his head with one of the throw pillows.

"It's worse than that, Josh. Only I'm not sure how." Katie was pacing around the room, thinking about everything that had just happened and trying to find a clue. A particularly loud scream made her look up. She shook her head. "Something strange is going on."

"He just doesn't like water," said Mrs. Lexington, coming downstairs a few minutes later and trying to smile. "But I *did* tell him to stand under that shower a long time." Mrs. Lexington lowered her voice. "He smells a lot better now, Josh, and he seemed very pleased that there were no fleas in the bed. He kept remarking on it. Hygiene must be very different over there. He didn't even bring a toothbrush!"

"Oh, Mom, why does he have to sleep in my room?" asked Josh.

"Yeah, it's not every day some weird kid in a costume shows up in the middle of the night to move in with us," added Katie.

"Ah, kids, it's just some new project of your mom's. Right, Betsy?" said Mr. Lexington, entering the room, pushing Josh's leg aside, and sitting next to him on the couch.

"That's exactly right, Abner," said Mrs. Lexington, squeezing in next to her husband. "Remember last summer how we wanted to go to Europe but we couldn't afford it?" Josh and Katie nodded their heads. "And how you kids were complaining all the time that you never got to go anywhere?"

"We *don't* get to go anywhere," muttered Josh.

"Well," continued Mrs. Lexington, ignoring him, "I decided that if we couldn't get to those countries, at least we could bring the countries — or rather, the people in them — to us. I signed us up as a host family for an exchange program. And it's free!"

"What? You mean you've adopted him?" yelled Josh. "This freaky sword-carrying kid is going to live with us?"

"No, no, no," soothed his mother, ruffling his hair. "He's here *visiting* us for just a month — and if all goes well, and you get along, maybe you'll get a chance to visit his family someday. It's an exchange program."

"What program, Betsy? I don't remember hearing anything about it." Mr. Lexington looked confused again.

"You know, Time Flyers. www.timeflyerkids. com. I found them on the Internet. And it was so easy to sign up." Mrs. Lexington was clearly very proud of herself.

"Time Flyers?" said Katie suspiciously. "Why 'Time Flyers'? That's a weird name for a student exchange program."

"*Time Flies when you host a Time Flyer!* That's their motto."

"Time Flyers?" asked Katie, still confused.

"That's what Time Flyers call their exchange students. And I think it's probably right. I can tell the next month with Jack is going to whiz by. Already, I've learned so much about England. Did you know that they still have outbreaks of the plague over there? The Black Death! Can you believe it?" Then, with a glance over her shoulder up the stairway, she added in a hushed voice, "Jack's mother died from it."

"The poor kid. That's just awful," sighed Mr. Lexington, shaking his head. "I'm glad we have the medical care we do in this country. It makes you realize how lucky we are to live in America." He wrapped an arm around his wife and gave her a squeeze. "Betsy, that boy's going to really appreciate having a mother to fuss over him this month."

"Oh, Abner, he's really very sweet. Such nice manners."

But Katie had found her clue. And she wasn't letting go of it. "The Black Death? Bubonic plague?" she said. "That hasn't been a problem for centuries. We read about it in social studies. You can treat it with antibiotics."

"That's what we're telling you, sweetie," said her father very seriously. "You're going to learn a lot about life in other parts of the world. It's just not the same as here."

Josh pulled the pillow off his face. "All I can say is, if I get some weird disease from this kid, you guys are going to pay. Will you ever owe me. You'll owe me big!"

"They still have the plague in England?" questioned Katie. "In *England*?"

"Yes, honey," answered her mother. "They may speak the same language, but they have a different way of life. C'mon, kids, let's get to bed. We'll have to be at school early tomorrow to get Jack signed in."

Josh and Katie followed their parents upstairs, but just as Josh was about to open the door to his room, Katie grabbed him by the arm. "Be quiet!" she whispered. "We've got work to do."

"Stop pinching me!"

"Shhh!" demanded Katie, and she held his arm tighter. She was watching the light under her parents' door. As soon as it was turned off, she pulled Josh into their mother's home office. "We've got to have a look at that Web site," she explained. "You listen and let me know if you hear anything."

"What's with all the secret agent stuff, Katie? Have you totally flipped?"

"Aren't you the least bit curious about what is going on?" asked Katie, turning on him. "Some strange kid shows up in the middle of the night in a costume, acting like you can still get the bubonic plague, asking for a glass of beer, talking like he's from some old-fashioned book, and Mom and Dad think it's perfectly normal. Don't you notice anything?"

"Do you think all kids from England smell that bad?"

"No, I don't. And I don't think he's from England, either."

Katie clicked on the computer in the dark and, while she waited for it to boot up, tapped her fingers impatiently against the screen.

"So what do you think?" said Josh. "Think someone's pulling a practical joke on us? 'Cause I'm telling you what, Katie, I don't want to bring this kid to school tomorrow."

"Wait a minute. Here we go. Look at this."

On the screen was a picture of an hourglass and the logo TIME FLYERS. Katie clicked on the site, and together she and Josh began reading about the joys of hosting students from different cultures. "Boring," sighed Josh, but Katie was scrolling down the page to an online application. There were all the typical questions about names and addresses and occupations. Katie stopped at a line that said "Time Preference."

"Time preference? What do you think that means?" she wondered aloud.

"You know," said Josh, "like do we want him to come in the summer or the fall or whatever."

"No," said Katie. "They asked that question earlier: *When would be the most convenient time for a visitor?* Why would they ask it again?"

Josh and Katie looked at each other, their faces lit by the glow from the computer. The house was completely quiet. They could hear each other breathing. In that moment they both had the same thought.

"He couldn't be from a different *time*, could he?" whispered Josh.

"Couldn't he?"

"But, I mean, it's not possible . . ."

"Not that we know . . ."

"Well, there's only one way to find out," said Josh, picking up a flashlight on his mother's desk. "Let's go."

Together they tiptoed into the hallway. Carefully, Katie eased open the door to Josh's bedroom. Josh shone the flashlight over the mess of clothes and papers and unfinished projects on the floor. The kid was under a mound of blankets on the lower bunk. Josh stopped the beam of light on a pile by the bed — Jack's clothes. Katie walked over and grabbed them. Then, together they hurried back out into the lighted hallway.

Up close, the clothes stank worse than ever. "Wow! I don't think these have ever been washed," said Josh.

Katie found a small leather pouch and opened it. "Yuck!" she said, pulling out an oozing piece of moldy cheese that had melted over some small silvery coins and a tiny golden hourglass.

"Let me see that!" Josh grabbed the hourglass from her hand and held it close to the flashlight. "Hey, Katie, this is really weird. The sand only falls . . ." Suddenly a voice came from the open doorway.

"Fie, ye knaves! Unhand my purse!"

Wearing Josh's own pajamas, sword drawn and pointed at Josh and Katie, stood Jack Bradford.

3 THE PLOT THICKENS

"Who *are* you?" demanded Josh.

"I am who I say — Jack Bradford of London. But ye be a scoundrel and a thief!"

"Shhh," warned Katie. "You'll wake Mom and Dad! Quick! Into the bedroom and shut the door." Stepping around the sword, she grabbed Jack by his pajamas and shoved him back into the bedroom. "C'mon! Now!" she whispered to her brother.

With the door shut, Katie flipped on the light. Jack and Josh glared at each other. "All right, everybody cool it. Jack, put that sword away. Josh, give that thing back to Jack, and both of you sit down," ordered Katie. "And I mean it!" She had her hands on her hips, and her face was red with rage.

Jack looked at her, then at Josh. "Is the poppet always this fierce?"

"Oh, man, she's the biggest pain who ever lived. She even used to bite!"

"Shut up, Josh!" snapped Katie, glaring at him.

"Okay, okay." He held out the hourglass to Jack, who took it, looked it over carefully, put it back in the small pouch, and laid his sword on the bureau. Both boys sat down on the floor. With his hair washed and wearing Josh's pajamas, Jack no longer looked so different from any other kid. Except for his long hair, he could have been a friend of Josh's.

But Katie was still standing over him like a lawyer at a trial. She said, "We want to know who you are and where you're from. The whole truth and nothing but the truth. Okay?"

"Okay? What means this 'okay'?"

Josh sighed, looked Jack over, and shook his head. "You're not from here, are you?"

"I am late of London, as I have said."

Josh had had enough. "Yeah, but what century? What year? What's all this Time Flyer stuff, anyway?"

Jack gasped. His eyes were wary. "It is not for me to say. On my honor I have sworn a solemn oath to reveal that truth to no man!"

"Well," said Katie, "I'm not a man."

"And neither am I," said Josh, then added hastily when Jack's face took on a look of surprise, "I mean, I'm just a kid."

Jack looked at them both. Katie could tell he wanted to say something, but he wasn't talking. He pulled at the cuff of his pajamas.

"Jack. Listen to me," pleaded Katie. "We're just kids and we've already figured out there's something wrong. Other people are going to, too — unless we help you."

Jack looked up into her eyes. He was biting his lip, clearly unsure of what to do. "Can you swear to me you will tell no one what I reveal to you?" he finally asked.

"I can more than swear," said Katie. "I'll make a pinkie promise."

"What?" said Jack.

"Here, give me your hand." Katie grabbed his hand and hooked her little finger around his. "Now," she said, "I swear I will never tell anyone where Jack is from."

"Me, too," added Josh, linking his pinkie to theirs at the last minute.

"Mayhap 'tis all right, then," he said to himself. He took a deep breath and turned to Katie. "Sit yourself down, maid. For I am to tell of wonders."

Katie looked at Josh. "I knew it!" she mouthed. She wrapped a blanket around herself and leaned in close as Jack began his story.

"No word I have said is a lie. I am Jack Bradford from London, from the England of Good Queen Bess" — and here he paused — "in the Year of Our Lord 1599."

"Yes!" said Katie. "I was right!"

"Wow!" said Josh. Then a look of horror crossed his face. "Oh, no. Wait'll Mom and Dad find out. They'll flip."

"Nay, nay, nay!" said Jack. "They must not!

You have promised me. For if they do, I must needs leave, says Master Dee."

"How are we gonna keep it from them, Katie?"

Katie gave her brother a look of complete disgust. "Do you think they notice anything — ever? Remember how long it took them to notice Iggy? How do you not notice a three-foot iguana?"

"Mom said she thought it was plastic."

"Exactly," nodded Katie. "Don't worry, Jack. Our parents are clueless. Your secret's safe with us."

"Katie's right," Josh agreed. "So how'd you get here, Jack?"

"After my mother did die last summer . . ."

"So your mother really did die of the plague?" interrupted Josh. Jack nodded his head and a shadow of sadness crossed his face.

"I'm sorry," said Katie.

"'Twas God's will," said Jack. "But home with my stepfather was no longer a place of comfort or fortune, so I made my way to London. There I found work with Master Dee, an apothecary. At first I carried messages for him, delivered vials of medicine, and swept his shop. But two nights ago, he awakened me in a most urgent voice and brought me into his room."

Jack leaned closer to Katie and Josh and lowered his voice to a whisper. "He shut the door, lit a candle, and then showed me a thin black box made of a strange metal. He lifted its lid, and marvelous pictures did appear on the face of the box, like a mirror that reflected an unknown world. It was then I realized Master Dee was a magician."

"Describe the box," said Josh.

"When Master Dee opened it, one side showed pictures. The other side, which lay flat, was covered with letters and numbers." Jack was clearly trying hard to remember. "'Twas by tapping these letters with his fingers that Master Dee did seem almost to command the pictures."

Josh looked at Katie, and they nodded at each other. "It almost sounds like a laptop to me," Josh said.

"Laptop?" questioned Jack.

"A computer," said Katie, and when Jack still

looked blank she went on. "A machine for information and thinking and, and . . ."

"Computers do everything for us," continued Josh. "We write letters on them, find stuff out, solve problems, whatever."

"And travel across time?" asked Jack.

"Well, no," answered Josh.

"Not yet, anyway," added Katie.

"Ah," said Jack. "Then it must be true what I have suspected about Master Dee."

"What's that?" asked Katie. But Jack ignored her question and went on with his story.

"Master Dee believed that my fortune could change forever if only I were to spend a month with a family of a different time. He warned me, however, that were any man to know of my origins, all could be ruined. It was then he had me swear a most dire and solemn oath. And at the last he showed me pictures of families, of mothers and fathers, and asked me to choose."

"And you chose us!" exclaimed Katie, smiling.

"Why?" asked Josh. "What's so special about us?"

Jack bowed his head. He seemed embarrassed. "Your mother's smile. It reminded me of my own mother's."

Neither Josh nor Katie said anything, so Jack continued. "Tonight Master Dee said the stars were arranged for my travels, and so I find myself here — to learn and explore."

"Welcome, Jack," said Katie.

The three children smiled at each other. Katie was proud of her detective work. Josh was realizing that life in the Lexington house was about to become a lot more interesting. And Jack was relieved to have made two friends in this strange land. The numbers on the digital clock on Josh's bureau nosily flipped over. It was midnight.

Katie stood up. "Well, we better get to sleep if we want to be ready for school tomorrow. Good night, you guys."

"Night, Katie. Hit the light, will ya?" said Josh. He turned to climb up into his bunk and then stopped. "Oh, GROSS! What's that in my soccer trophy?"

Beside the bed was Joshua's enormous,

gold-plated soccer trophy with the fancy handles. It was filled with a foul-smelling yellow liquid.

"Is that not the chamber pot?" asked Jack.

"Chamber pot? *Chamber pot?* Is that what you think it is? You went to the bathroom in my soccer trophy?" Josh was yelling again.

Poor Jack looked lost. "What would you have me do? Use the floor?"

Katie came between them again. "Jack, we have toilets. C'mon. Josh will show you how they work. But from now on," and even though she was littler than he was, she took him by both arms and turned him around to look at her, "you better remember you're in the twenty-first century. You don't do anything, and I mean *anything*, without checking with us first!"

4 AUDITIONS

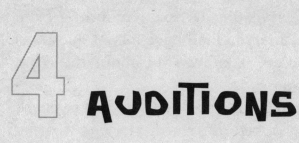

Jack was placed in Mrs. Pitney's class after a long morning of filling out forms in the principal's office with Mrs. Lexington. Katie and Josh had prepped him when they found out he hadn't been to school in three years.

"Don't tell them," commanded Josh. "Just say you're in sixth grade like me. All kids go to school these days. And since it's the beginning of the year, you'll fit in fine." But Josh felt the knot in his stomach getting tighter and tighter while he and Jack walked down the hall.

Mrs. Pitney, a small woman with battleship-gray hair cut short around her ears, introduced Jack to the class. "Attention, everyone. This is Jack

Bradford. He's visiting us for a month — from England. I'm sure you'll all have lots of questions for him at recess. I know I do about the royal family!"

All the girls and boys leaned forward to check out Jack. He looked awkward. He was wearing jeans Josh had lent him, but he kept pulling at them. "A man's legs cannot breathe in these," he'd complained.

Josh slumped down in his chair, holding his breath and hoping Jack wouldn't do anything strange. At least he didn't smell like an old trash can anymore.

"Jack, is there anything you'd like to say to the class?" asked Mrs. Pitney.

Jack took a deep breath and stood up straight. "*Salve, Magistera. Spero me dignum discipulum fore.* . . . Madam, I apologize. My Latin is poor. And my Greek worse." He bowed his head, obviously embarrassed.

"No, no, Jack. Very nice. I think you'll be raising our educational standards here at Alice R. Quigley Middle School, won't he, class?" Everyone groaned, especially Evan Ferrante, who sat behind Josh. "Stuck-up show-off," he whispered to Frank Lubka. Frank nodded and cracked his knuckles.

Jack sat at the desk next to Josh's. His eyes opened wide as Mrs. Pitney placed textbooks, paper, and a pen in front of him. "Truly, this pen is a marvel!" he whispered to Josh. And during writing workshop he hummed to himself and covered the paper with elaborate flourishes and curlicues. After they turned in their papers, however, Mrs. Pitney called Jack up to her desk.

"Jack, your spelling. It's very . . . uh . . . creative."

"Yes, mistress. Why, I can spell my own name six different ways." He gave Mrs. Pitney a big grin.

"Really?" Mrs. Pitney's eyebrows were coming closer together under her glasses and she wasn't smiling.

"Aye. Shall I show ye?" Jack grabbed a piece of chalk, as he had seen Mrs. Pitney do, and scrawled on the blackboard, "Jacke, Jak, Jake, Jaek, Jac, Jack." He turned back to the class and bowed. A number of the girls giggled. Lizzie Markle passed Josh a note. "He is *soooo* cute!" it said.

"That will be enough, Jack." Mrs. Pitney stood up and glared at Jack, who didn't seem to notice. "I am impressed when people know how to spell words correctly."

"But how do ye know? Surely there is no book to say what is right? Is not a word's play all in its spelling?"

For a moment Mrs. Pitney was speechless. Then she picked up a large book from her desk and said icily, "May I recommend the dictionary, Jack?" Frank Lubka snickered.

For the rest of the morning Jack kept quiet, but as soon as they were out in the hallway for lunch, he turned to Josh and announced, "Your mistress is quite witless, Josh. No Latin in her class. No dancing. 'Tis what comes of letting a female addle her brain with learning." He leaned back against a locker, looked around, and tugged at Josh's arm to bring him closer. "But," he said, pointing at a group of girls clustered around the water fountain, "I am much for this innovation of maids in school."

But Josh wasn't looking at the girls. He'd noticed Frank and Evan and a couple of their friends huddled together and laughing. They were planning something. He knew it.

"C'mon, Jack. Let's get lunch. It's spaghetti today."

"*Spaghetti?* What is *spaghetti?*"

"You'll see," Josh said and pulled him along to the cafeteria.

They got their trays, and Jack followed behind Josh, taking everything that he did. Entering the crowded room, they saw the tables were full. Josh was looking for his friend Neil Carmody, who always saved him a seat, when Frank Lubka deliberately bumped into Jack and sent his tray of spaghetti flying across the room.

"Hey, watch where you're going, freak!" sneered Frank.

"Yeah!" said Evan Ferrante, pushing him from behind. "You got your nose so high in the air, you ain't lookin' where you're goin'."

35

"What, sirrah? Why, thou art a boil and a plague sore! By my beard not yet grown in, thou shalt pay for it!" Jack stepped up close to Frank and spit on him.

"Hey, you *spit* on me!" said Frank, wiping his face.

"Shall we fight at dawn, then? To the death?"

Kids were dropping their lunches to get a better look. Someone began a chant of "fight, fight, fight, fight . . ."

"Hey, man, just get away from us, okay?" said Evan, stepping back.

"That kid's psycho!" said Frank.

"Nay, you cur! Thou cannot excuse the injuries that thou hast done me! Name thy weapon!"

"No!" screamed Josh, remembering the sword from the night before and jumping in front of Jack. Jack was red-faced and breathing hard. "Help! Somebody help!" yelled Josh.

From across the room, Mr. Tufnell, the drama teacher, came running. "Now, now, boys!" he said.

"That new kid picked a fight!" shouted someone.

"He *spit* on me!" screamed Frank.

"Oh, dear! Oh, dear!" said Mr. Tufnell as he pushed through the crowd.

Josh shut his eyes. All morning long he'd had a terrible feeling something was going to go wrong. Jack would get kicked out of school. *He'd* get kicked out of school. Secret government agents would be swarming all over their house before you knew it, his mother and father would be taken away for questioning. . . . He opened his eyes, fearing the worst. There was Katie standing between Mr. Tufnell and Jack.

"Hi, Mr. Tufnell!" she said cheerfully. "This is Jack Bradford, our new exchange student. Isn't he a great actor?" Mr. Tufnell looked at her and rubbed his eyes. "You know, Mr. Tufnell, the fight scene in *Romeo and Juliet*? He's acting it out, isn't he?" Katie glared at Jack, stepping hard on his foot with her heel. "Isn't that right, Jack?"

She smiled again at Mr. Tufnell. "You know, Mr. Tufnell, Jack was telling me just this morning how much he loves acting." Josh saw her reach out and pinch Jack hard behind her back. "He wants to be in the play. I mean, this wasn't the best way to try out, was it, Jack?" She pinched him again, and he gasped and swatted at her hand. "But it was still a pretty good audition. Right, Mr. Tufnell?"

"Well, we *do* need boys for the play. . . ." said Mr. Tufnell, looking at Jack in a whole new way.

"He'd make a great Romeo, wouldn't he?"

"Yes. Yes. I think you're right."

"Okay, everybody, show's over!" announced Katie. "Back to lunch!"

"So, Jack, tell me," said Mr. Tufnell, stepping close and peering at him, "have you ever been in a play before?"

5 THE CAST OF CHARACTERS

When Josh brought Jack into the auditorium after school, a group of girls were dropping their backpacks by the stage. They all looked up and stopped talking when Jack walked into the room. Josh found Katie and pulled her aside.

"Keep an eye on him, will ya? All afternoon he kept flicking his thumb at Evan and Frank. Whatever he was doing, it wasn't a compliment, and they knew it. Plus, Lizzie Markle is after him. Look!" Josh pointed across the auditorium where the curly-haired girl was leaning up close to Jack and giggling.

"You mean you're not staying for rehearsal?" asked Katie.

"Rehearsal? For your stupid play? I'm out of here!" And Josh hurried out the door as fast as he could to catch his bus.

"We're so excited you're going to be in the play with us, Jack," Lizzie was saying when Katie came over. "I can't wait to hear more about England. You know, I'm a huge expert on Princess Di."

"Did the princess die? Which princess?" Jack looked very upset.

"Excuse me, Lizzie," interrupted Katie. "C'mon, Jack, help me set up these chairs before Mr. Tufnell gets here." Jack followed Katie up onto the stage and started helping her arrange some folding chairs in a circle. "Watch out for Lizzie, okay, Jack?" she whispered to him. "That girl is trouble — she's not as stupid as she looks."

Mr. Tufnell arrived moments later, holding a dripping cup of coffee in one hand and a pile of scripts in the other. "Girls, girls, it's time to start," he announced.

As the girls, giggling and chattering, took their seats, Jack looked around the auditorium. "But where are the players?" he asked. He looked concerned.

"Players?" said Lizzie. "Is that what you call them in England? We call them actors or actresses — and we're all right here." She pulled Jack down in the seat next to her.

"Mr. Tufnell better give me a good part. He's posting the parts today, you know," she said to him, resting her hand on his shoulder. "I always star in the school plays. You're going to be Romeo, aren't you? I just know it."

But Jack ignored her. "Why, this cannot be!" yelled Jack so loudly that Mr. Tufnell spilled his coffee all over the scripts. "'Tis against the law for maids to act upon a stage. Your theater shall be shut down!"

"What are you talking about?" said Lizzie. "The only ones who *want* to be in school plays are the girls." All the girls nodded their heads. "I mean, you're the only boy we've been able to get. And I'm telling you, I am not playing a boy. No way."

"Well, I'm not, either!" said Vanessa Foster. "What would I do with my hair?"

All at once everyone started arguing and had completely forgotten what Jack had said. Lizzie and Vanessa were both insisting that they should play Juliet; two fifth-graders announced they were thinking of quitting if they didn't get a good part; and Sylvia Macavoy was wondering why Mr. Tufnell had picked such a stupid play, anyway. "Why can't we do *Cats*?" she whined.

"Now, girls, girls!" piped up Mr. Tufnell, waving his coffee-covered hands in the air. "Silence, everyone! Silence, please! Now, Jack, what was it you were saying?"

But Jack was looking around the room, nodding his head and smiling. "Ah, I see, I see! 'Tis no longer unseemly for girls to strut and play. I like this century! I do!"

"Century?" Lizzie said under her breath.

"But why do you complain?" continued Jack. "Why, a true actor should be glad of any part, should he not? What care he if he wear a dress or carry a sword, so long as the lines be good and the story bold? If men can play maids, why not maids men?"

"Hear! Hear!" said Katie. "I want one of the boy's parts. I want to be Romeo's friend Mercutio! So there!"

"Who's Mercutio?" said Vanessa.

"He is Romeo's best friend," answered Jack, smiling at Katie.

"What's this play about, anyway?" asked Lizzie.

"Oh!" said Mr. Tufnell, taken aback. "Doesn't everyone know the story of *Romeo and Juliet* already?" Most of the girls shook their heads, and the rest looked blankly at him.

"Well, then, I guess I'd better tell you." Mr. Tufnell took a big breath and a sip of coffee, and then looked around the room at all the girls. "Romeo, that's the boy. Montague is his last name. Or is it Capulet? Oh, dear, oh, dear . . ." Mr. Tufnell started to sigh and fumble through one of the scripts.

Jack cleared his throat. "Master. 'Tis Montague. Romeo Montague, the only child of a noble family in fair Verona."

"Oh!" squeaked Mr. Tufnell. "Do you know Shakespeare, Jack?"

"Aye. I met Master Will once at the Crown and Thorn. He was in fine spirits."

Mr. Tufnell looked confused for a moment. "Oh. I don't remember that part of the play." And then his face brightened. "But maybe you can tell the girls the story?"

"I would be honored to. I have seen the play six times and know great parts of it by heart."

Jack stood and bowed, and Lizzie giggled again. He began explaining the plot of Shakespeare's play. As he did so, he seemed to forget himself and become each of the characters he described.

He told of the two families who hated each other. He pretended to be Romeo and his friends sneaking into a party at the enemy Capulet's house and seeing Juliet Capulet for the first time. When he told of Romeo and Juliet dancing together, he danced around the stage and then kissed his hand toward an imaginary girl. Lizzie and Vanessa sighed at the same moment.

He stood on a chair, playing Juliet in the famous balcony scene. "Oh, Romeo, Romeo," he said in a high-pitched voice. "Wherefore art thou, Romeo?" Then he bent over and seemed to shrivel up and become Juliet's old nurse warning her about Romeo, a Montague, and therefore Juliet's enemy. All the girls and Mr. Tufnell, too, were amazed by his performance.

During the sword-fighting scenes, he dashed from one side of the auditorium to the other. He fell to the floor when Mercutio was killed, and again when Romeo killed Juliet's cousin. A few girls sniffled and wiped their eyes when Romeo began to say his final lines before dying.

"*Thus with a kiss I die!*" Jack proclaimed, and he was just about to fall over dead, when the thud of a backpack hitting the floor made him look up.

"Am I late?" Standing at the entrance to the auditorium was a breathless girl with dark eyes and shiny auburn hair that fell to her waist. "I'm really sorry, but I had to make sure that my brother Frank showed up for detention today."

"*What light through yonder window breaks?*" whispered Jack.

"Oh, no," said Katie to herself.

"Cynthia Lubka," said Mr. Tufnell. "I thought you'd never make it! Jack, meet your Juliet."

6 LINES TO LEARN

"Joshua Lexington, you have to!"

"I don't want to be in the play, Mom. Everyone will make fun of me. Everyone knows Mr. Tufnell puts on the worst plays ever. Besides, Katie's there with him." Josh was arguing with his mother in the kitchen after school. Katie and Jack, just home from rehearsal, watched TV in the living room.

"It's only for a month," insisted Mrs. Lexington. "Besides, Jack doesn't have any friends here other than you and Katie. Rehearsals won't interfere with soccer practice. I'm calling the school right now and leaving a message with that dear Mr. Tufnell. I don't know what your problem with him is. Jack's our guest and it's the polite thing to do." Mrs. Lexington picked up the telephone and Josh groaned.

Josh had still not recovered from his day at school. After the near-fight at lunch, he spent all afternoon covering for Jack. During science class Jack had insisted that the sun revolved around the earth, and he denied, in a loud voice, that man had landed on the moon. And to top it all off, snoopy Lizzie Markle was passing Jack notes, and on the way home, in the back of the bus, he could hear Frank and Evan snickering. How could he do this for a month? He thought at least he'd get to relax after school. No such luck.

"There. All done," his mother said, hanging up the phone. "Now how about a 'spot of tea' for everyone?" Mrs. Lexington said with an English accent. "I thought it would be nice if we had tea and crumpets in the afternoon while Jack is here — just like they do in England."

She picked up a tray, and Josh followed her into the other room. Katie was sitting on a chair, her schoolbooks spread around her, looking at the TV occasionally. Jack, however, was standing up, his hands clenched in fists, yelling at the wide screen. "No, sirrah, thou art a black dog."

"Jack, a crumpet?" interrupted Mrs. Lexington, holding the tray out to him.

Jack looked at the pile of muffins on the plate, grabbed one, and hurled it at the television.

"Jack!" exclaimed Mrs. Lexington.

"Madam! Look at this cur!" he shouted, pointing at one of the characters. "He is a churl! A blackguard!" He grabbed another crumpet and threw it.

"Chill out!" said Josh, grabbing his arm. "It's just a sitcom."

"Jack, we do not throw our food in this house." Mrs. Lexington had a smile on her face, but she meant business.

"Look, Jack. It's TV," said Katie, glaring at him. "Sit down." Jack sat.

Mrs. Lexington sighed and put the tea tray on the table. "There, that's better. Help yourselves, kids. I'm going to get dinner ready."

As soon as she was out of the room, Katie turned to Jack. "What were you doing?"

"I was watching this telling vision with you."

"No," said Katie. "I mean what's all the throwing and yelling about?"

"Is that not the sport of a play? To shout and yell? That's what we do at the Globe."

"Jack. You don't move when you watch TV," instructed Josh. "Watch me. You sit down and veg out." Josh sprawled across the couch, let his eyes glaze over, and his mouth drop open. Then he looked at Jack. "Just be a couch potato, okay?"

Jack looked confused but sat down on the couch and arranged himself to look as bored as Josh. Every now and then, something would happen on TV and he'd get excited again, but he would look at Josh and collapse. At one point, he reached over and poured himself a cup of tea, tasted it, and spat it out. "What is this vile drink?"

"Tea," said Katie. "Don't tell me you've never had it before?"

Jack, afraid to speak, just shook his head. Katie sighed. "Don't tell Mom."

At one point, Jack pulled from his pocket the tiny hourglass that Katie and Jack had seen the night before. Tiny grains of golden sand were slowly falling from the top to the bottom. But when Jack flipped the hourglass over, instead of changing direction, the falling sand continued to flow — now up instead of down. Jack put it back in his pocket before either Katie or Josh noticed.

That night at dinner, Mr. Lexington was delighted to discover that both boys would be in the play. "I'll tell you, kids, I was a bit of an actor in my day. In sixth grade I even played the father of our country in *Georgie, Grab Your Musket.*"

"And you were wonderful. I still remember that uniform," said Mrs. Lexington, spooning more green beans onto her plate.

"But, Dad," said Josh. "None of the guys try out for school plays anymore. Everyone's going to think I'm a nerd."

Mrs. Lexington looked knowingly at her husband, who nodded. Clearly, they'd already had a talk.

"Son," said Mr. Lexington, "I think it's an opportunity. Why, look what acting did for Arnold

Schwarzenegger, for Ronald Reagan. Where would they have been without their acting careers?"

"By your leave, gentle sir," interrupted Jack, "who are these men of whom you speak?"

Mr. Lexington put down his fork. "You don't know who Ronald Reagan was? Or the Terminator?" Jack shook his head. "Wow, Jack. You really are from a different country, aren't you?"

Katie rushed in to help. "They were both movie actors, Jack. Reagan became President of our country, and Schwarzenegger became governor of California."

"Players became leaders, men of power?"

"Oh, yes," added Mrs. Lexington. "And rich, too. Well, they were rich to begin with. You must have actors in government in England?"

"Nay, madam!" Jack looked almost stunned. "Most players are thought of as thieves and scoundrels. At best they are ta'en for rogues and ne'er-do-wells."

"Really?" said Mrs. Lexington, looking surprised. "We just love actors in America. I'll have to get you a *People* magazine while you're here. Remind me, kids, will you?"

Both Josh and Katie were staring at Jack. He wore a strange expression on his face, but he didn't look upset — he looked, thought Katie, almost inspired.

Later, up in Josh's room, Jack confided to them his secret dream. He wanted to be an actor back home in England. "Always when I find myself with a penny, I take myself to the theater. Some may prefer a bearbaiting or a hanging, but I — I love a play!" His eyes were sparkling. "Yet ne'er did I e'en dare imagine that I, too, could be one of them. Always I thought 'twould dishonor my fair mother's memory to be a mere player."

"Well, I'm with your mother, Jack," said Josh from the top bunk. "No matter what my parents say, it's gonna dishonor my rep in school to be in one of Tufnell's plays."

"Oh, shut up!" said Katie, throwing a pillow at him. She turned back to Jack. "So you think your mom wouldn't mind you being in a play now?"

"Not if in the future it leads to such greatness," said Jack. "Look at your parents — how proud they are of us that we are in a play. Yea, verily, I am resolved, when I return home I shall work to become one of The Lord Chamberlain's Men with Will Shakespeare." And he reached into his pocket, wrapping his fingers around the hourglass.

7 DIRECTOR'S CUT

Jack took *Romeo and Juliet* very seriously. On the bus and in the hallways his script was always open as he studied his lines. In Mrs. Pitney's class he would sometimes forget himself and answer a question with words from the play. When she asked him about photosynthesis, all he could say was, "*A rose by any other name would smell as sweet.*"

He was also always getting caught off guard and expressing amazement at some ordinary aspect of daily life in the twenty-first century. On the day Mrs. Pitney handed him a calculator during math, he exclaimed, "O brave new world that has such wonders in it! If only I'd had this when I was a student, I should have soared with success. No sum would have been too hard for me!"

"I suppose your teachers in England don't let you use calculators, Jack," said Mrs. Pitney.

"Nay, madam. We must figure columns of numbers for hours and hours."

"Well, perhaps that explains why you are so behind in math. It quite surprised me how little work you've done in math and the sciences. I always thought of foreigners being ahead of us, but apparently that is not so. Back to work, class!"

Jack wasn't getting very good grades. And at rehearsal when he wasn't performing, instead of doing his homework, he would sit and gaze at Cynthia Lubka.

"*She doth teach the torches to burn bright*," he murmured while watching her brush out her hair.

"I hope you're just practicing your lines," said Josh, who was sitting next to him. He'd been cast in a small part as one of Romeo's friends but spent most of his time at rehearsals helping to paint the scenery.

"Oh, Joshua. I no longer know. She hath cast a spell over me."

"Well, just watch out, okay? Or her brother Frank's gonna cast something a lot worse over you." Josh knew that Evan and Frank were pretty scared of Jack. Still, Josh had seen the expression on Frank's face when Jack had tried to sit with Cynthia on the bus, and both Frank and Evan were now lurking around after school. Mostly they hung out in the hallway bouncing a basketball back and forth. But the moment rehearsal was over, Frank would rush in and grab his sister by the arm to take her home.

The first week of rehearsal, the girls sat around braiding each other's hair onstage. Mr. Tufnell kept forgetting where he put his script, and everyone would have to run around and look for it. And Lizzie Markle was determined to do a different play. She had been cast as Juliet's old nurse — and she was furious. "I don't know why you chose such a stupid play, Mr. Tufnell. I really don't. Maybe we should just do a lip sync instead."

"Yeah," added Vanessa. "Why can't we just do a play in English, anyway? Nobody knows what they are saying. It's boring."

"The words of Will Shakespeare, boring? Fie upon you!" yelled Jack from across the room. "'Tis no different from these sitting comedies and soaping operas that you watch. Only there is greater laughter and greater feeling. Come, I will show you."

Jack called all the girls around and began translating the Elizabethan swears and jokes into American English. "When you say you bite your thumb at them, you are really saying . . ." and he stopped for a moment to make sure Mr. Tufnell wasn't listening and whispered an explanation.

"Oh!" said the girls, their eyes widening.

"Oh!" said Josh and Katie, nodding their heads. Josh whispered to Katie, "I think Evan and Frank figured that out."

The next week, Jack began conducting swordfighting lessons, showing everyone how to thrust and parry. He taught dancing classes for the party scene. He even convinced Mr. Tufnell to play the old friar in the play. "You are perfect for the part," he said, and Mr. Tufnell blushed. Everyone loved what Jack told them to do — except Lizzie.

Whenever Jack and Cynthia were doing a scene together, Lizzie would sit on the edge of the stage rolling her eyes every time Cynthia spoke. Cynthia was perfect as Juliet. She was one of the prettiest girls at Alice R. Quigley Middle School, and Jack couldn't keep his eyes off her. It was becoming clearer and clearer, too, that Cynthia had a crush on him as well. Nothing made Lizzie more furious than when the two of them had to kiss during a scene. She'd cross her arms, getting madder and madder, and one day she even snorted out loud when they were holding hands.

"I've been thinking," Lizzie interrupted them one afternoon during the third week of rehearsals. "I think we're missing a really important part of this play."

Jack and Cynthia both turned to look at her, but they kept their hands clasped together. Jack looked irritated.

"You know, I think the nurse is really young and beautiful. And, I mean, couldn't she *also* be in love with Romeo? Romeo could really be in love with her, too, and only be using Juliet to get close to the nurse."

"The nurse?" said Cynthia. "But the nurse has cared for Juliet her whole life. She's more her mother than her real mother."

"But Juliet is only thirteen!" said Lizzie. "So . . . so . . . the nurse, I mean, maybe she's like, you know, twenty."

"Nay! Nay! The nurse is a hag!" yelled Jack, infuriated. "There's the jest! The laughter. All of Romeo's friends do mock the nurse because she is so ugly and old. Juliet is young and beautiful. The nurse is wrinkled and warty. Always when I have seen this play, the ugliest and oldest man in the company hath played the part."

"Are you saying I look like an old man?" fumed Lizzie, turning on Jack. There was fire in her eyes.

"Oh, Lizzie, just give it a rest, will you?" snapped Katie.

"So now little Miss Perfect is giving me directions, too? Well, I have had enough. So long, Mr. T. Let me know if you ever decide to do a *real* play." Lizzie grabbed her backpack and stormed out into the hallway.

"Good riddance!" said Katie.

But Josh wasn't so sure. He'd known Lizzie ever since preschool. If there was one thing you could count on with her, it was that she always got her way. He heard the basketball stop thumping out in the hallway. *Oh, no!* he thought. But just as he was about to share his fears with Katie, he noticed that Jack and all the girls were staring at him.

"What?" he said, looking up.

"As it please you, Josh," Jack was saying, "now Lizzie has left, we will need you to take a different part."

"What part? I already learned my line for the one I've got."

"'Tis a fine role, Josh. The groundlings always love it. You are the one to make them laugh," said Jack. Katie started to giggle.

Josh began to understand and he didn't like it. "No way! No way! Forget it. Just forget it. It's bad enough that I'm even in this play. I'm not playing the nurse. She's a girl!"

"She's not a girl, Josh, she's an old lady," said Katie. "You'd make a great old nurse with warts. I've always thought so!" She burst out laughing.

"Can't somebody else do it?" pleaded Josh, looking around.

"No, Josh," said Mr. Tufnell, speaking up. "We're so close to performance. We only have another week to go and everybody else has already learned their lines."

"Nah," said Josh, shaking his head. "I'm sorry, guys, but someone else is gonna have to do it."

"Friend," said Jack, putting his hand on Josh's arm. "You must. All that I wish for depends on the success of this play. If it is to fail, why, certainly all shall fail for me at home."

Josh looked at Jack, and for a moment he thought about life back in England in 1599, a place where your mom could die of the plague, your stepdad could kick you out of the house when you were only twelve, everybody carried a sword, and nobody took a bath. "All right, Jack," he sighed. "I'll do it for you. Because you're my friend. But you owe me. You owe me big-time!"

62

8 BACKSTAGE

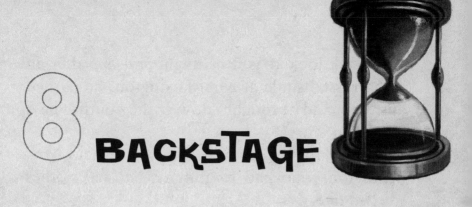

The last weekend before the performance, Mrs. Lexington was busy at home making costumes for the show. Jack was fascinated by her sewing machine.

"Ah, if my mother had such a device, how much easier her life would have been. So many nights I watched her up late darning and mending by candlelight. And then, no more."

Mrs. Lexington's eyes welled up with tears for a moment at Jack's words. "Dear, I noticed when you came that some of your clothes were a little torn. Why don't you bring them down to me and I'll get them all fixed up for you before you go." She reached out and patted Jack on the arm.

Now Jack looked as if he might cry, but after an embarrassed smile at Mrs. Lexington, he dashed upstairs and brought down the outfit he'd arrived in.

"Well, maybe a dry cleaning first," said Mrs. Lexington, who had forgotten what the clothes smelled like.

At dress rehearsal the following week, Mrs. Lexington arrived at the auditorium with the enormous box of costumes she'd made. On the top of the box were Jack's clothes, which he was going to wear as a costume — cleaned, ironed, and newly sewn. He looked at them in amazement. "Madam, you have worked wonders with them."

Mrs. Lexington blushed and then bustled about handing the other children their costumes. "Now, don't panic if they don't fit. I've got plenty of safety pins," she said. She handed out capes and tights and gowns. To Josh, she handed three large pillows with a belt sewn onto them.

"What's this?" he said, holding it up.

"That's your padding, dear. When Jack and I

were working on the designs together, he suggested it."

"You mean in addition to being a girl and old, I'm also gonna be fat?" But at this point he knew better than to resist. He strapped the pillows around his waist and began trying on his dress, muttering under his breath the whole time. "I mean, I am never, ever gonna live this down."

It had been a tough week for Josh. At recess he had caught Mrs. Pitney cornering Jack with questions about the royal family. "So what do you like best about the queen?" she was saying. Jack was just starting to talk about how she'd really cut back on the burnings and beheadings, when Josh managed to distract Mrs. Pitney with a made-up math question.

He and Katie had to take turns keeping an eye on Frank and Evan — and now Lizzie. The three of them had clearly teamed up and spent a lot of time huddled together plotting *something*. Josh and Katie kept trying to sneak up behind them and hear what they were saying.

Plus, Josh still had so many lines to learn. As soon as he was in his costume and his mother had plopped a huge hat on him that wrapped around his head and covered his ears, he sat down and went back to memorizing his last speech. *"Alas, alas! Help, help! My lady's dead!"* he kept saying over and over again in a high-pitched voice. It was easy for him to focus. He could barely hear anything with his hat on — including the giggles of the other cast members when they looked at him.

Jack loved the costumes. "Madam Lexington, you are a marvel!" he exclaimed, looking at Cynthia in a blue velvet gown.

Mrs. Lexington blushed, "Jack, you are too sweet. But you're sure you don't mind wearing tights?"

"Nay, madam!" said Jack, stretching his legs. "'Tis good to be able to flex my knees again. I have had enough of blue jeans."

"He really gets into the part, doesn't he?" said Mrs. Lexington to Katie.

Katie smiled indulgently at her mother. "He's an amazing actor — and a director, too. We couldn't have done this play without him."

Mr. Tufnell had just appeared, pulling at his black robes and clapping his hands. "All right, actors! Places! Places! We need to begin the dress rehearsal!"

Everyone began moving backstage — except Josh, who was having trouble getting up off the floor. "C'mon, bro," said Katie, giving him a hand and laughing. He started to swat her, but she leaped away. Josh could barely move with his long skirt and pillows bouncing all around him.

The lights dimmed, the curtain rose, and the dress rehearsal began. Mrs. Lexington, the only person in the audience, clapped enthusiastically.

When he wasn't onstage, Jack stood in the wings, watching and taking notes. Swords slashed and skirts swirled. But just as Jack began to climb up to Juliet's balcony, the entire auditorium went completely black. Pitch-black.

"Someone hit the lights!" shouted Mr. Tufnell.

"I am and nothing's working," yelled the seventh-grader who was working the light board.

"Where's the switch?" asked someone.

"That's not working, either!" said a voice.

Mr. Tufnell groped along the wall toward the outside door and opened it. Light from parking lot lamps flooded into the room, and the cast raced outside. Even though it was night and the stars were out, it was still lighter than it was in the blackened auditorium. Mr. Tufnell was trying to catch his breath as he consulted his attendance roster. ". . . Jack. Yes. Vanessa. Yes. Cynthia. Yes. . . . Oh, thank goodness, we're all here."

"Good," said Katie. "I'll just be a second." She had a feeling she knew who was behind the darkness. Sure enough, she raced around the side of the building just in time to see Frank and Evan running out the front door and down the street. "Come back here!" she shouted after them, but they didn't even turn around.

By the time she got back to the others, Mr. Conway, the school custodian, was talking to Mr. Tufnell. "I'm sure it's just a fuse, kids. I'll have it fixed in a jiffy." A few minutes later, the lights were on again and Mr. Conway was herding them all back into the building.

"I should have realized they'd try to pull something tonight," said Katie to Josh. "But if that's all they could think of, we're lucky."

Everyone returned to the auditorium and picked up where they had left off. The play went on without a hitch. During the curtain calls, Mrs. Lexington leaped to her feet and started shouting, "Bravo! Bravo!" Jack bowed again and then put up his hands to stop her. "Peace, peace, Madame Lexington."

Soon kids were handing their costumes back to Mrs. Lexington, who hung them up in the changing room. "Pants! Hooray!" said Josh, stepping back into his.

"Have you seen my blue jeans and shirt, Josh?" asked Jack.

"Weren't they on the chair?"

"I thought I did leave them there, but now they are vanished."

Josh and Jack began hunting around the room

for the missing pants and shirt. Soon the whole cast was on a hunt for Jack's missing clothes, searching through the seats in the auditorium, in the bathrooms, behind the sets — but they were nowhere to be found.

"I must find them!" cried Jack, looking around the room wildly.

"Well, Jack," said Mrs. Lexington, throwing up her hands. "You'll just have to wear your costume home. We'll find your clothes tomorrow."

"Nay! Nay! Nay!" yelled Jack, desperately. "I must find them now!"

"I guess he's started to like jeans," commented Josh to Katie.

Parents began arriving and the girls picked up their things and headed home. Mr. Tuffnell was putting some last dabs of paint on the scenery and humming to himself. But Jack was still upset.

Cynthia was patting him on the arm, trying to calm him down. "It'll be okay, Jack. You look so cool in your costume."

"This seems like Lizzie's work," said Katie. "I

bet she stole Jack's clothes while everything was dark. I should have suspected something."

"But it's just clothes," said Josh.

"Alack the day!" moaned Jack. "Alack the day!"

All the way home in the car, Jack kept sighing and groaning and looking out the window. Mrs. Lexington kept trying to reassure him with promises that she'd buy him a new pair of jeans first thing tomorrow. But nothing helped.

Only later, when the Lexingtons had gone to bed, and Katie had joined the boys in their bedroom, did they discover what was really the matter.

"'Tis not the clothes!" said Jack when the door was shut. "'Tis what was in them."

"Oh," said Josh and Katie together.

"I was not supposed to let you see it, but I must tell you for what I search. You must help me find it. You must!"

"What is it?" asked Josh.

"Before I left, Master Dee gave me an hour-glass."

"I remember that!" interrupted Josh. "I saw it the first day you arrived. I totally forgot about it."

"Master Dee told me to keep it with me always. When the sand is flowing one way, I am here. When it runs out and goes in the other direction, I will leave. But only if *I* am holding it. If Evan or Frank or Lizzie is holding it, I will remain here, and they will return to England in 1599."

"Perfect!" said Josh. "What're the chances of them getting beheaded, do you think?"

"Awesome!" said Katie. "It would be great if Lizzie Markle never got to take a bath again! Just think what her hair would look like!"

"This is terrific, Jack! Now you can stay with us," added Josh.

But Jack didn't look happy. He was fighting them back, but big tears were welling up in his eyes.

"Oh, friends," he finally said. "Would that I could and be content. What have I to return to, you may ask. No family, few friends, little fortune. But there is so much I have missed and ached for while I am here — the taste of a warm sop in the morn, the sound of the gossips on the street, the smell of . . ."

"What? You miss the *smells*? You gotta be kidding me!"

"Nay, Josh. Yours is a strangely odorless world. But it is more than that even. 'Tis the excitement at the Globe before the play begins — the nobles arriving, the groundlings hurrying in, the orange sellers hawking their wares, and the thrill when the players take the stage. Were I to stay here, I would have to mope and dawdle in school for years and years. I cannot sit here as this couch vegetable — nay, not while in London Master Shakespeare opens a new play! 'Twould be exile. At home, I need bother no longer with lessons. I have decided that when I return, I will ask Master Dee to leave his service and begin an apprenticeship in the theater. London is my home and I must needs go back."

"How do you get back, anyway?" asked Josh.

"'Tis magic."

"You don't know how it works?"

"I am not a magician. I cannot change how anything happens."

"Has anyone there been missing you?" asked Katie.

Jack gave Katie a long look and quietly shook his head. "Master Dee is the only soul I know in London. But still it is home, and I must return."

"And you will," said Katie. "We'll get through the play tomorrow night and then we'll start searching for that hourglass. . . ."

"Nay! Nay! We must find it now! There are but a few grains left to fall. I think soon after the performance 'twill be the time. I have been here almost a month, after all."

"Has it been that long?" questioned Josh.

"Wow. Time really does fly with a Time Flyer," said Katie.

"And there be almost no time left," said Jack.

9 OPENING NIGHT

Josh was all for sneaking over to the Lubkas' house with flashlights and searching Frank's bedroom in the dark. Jack thought that was an excellent idea and wanted to bring his sword. But Katie had other plans.

"No. Lizzie must have the hourglass. I'm almost sure of it. She took the pants. I'll bet she's the brains of this operation."

"So we should go to her house?" asked Josh.

"Oh, Josh," said Katie, looking at her brother with disgust. "You really think we can walk a mile to her house after midnight, bypass their family's alarm system, and find a tiny hourglass in Lizzie's bedroom without waking her up? This isn't a spy

75

movie. It won't work. We've got to find a way to trick it out of her."

Katie looked at Jack and Josh. "But the real question is, what did she want when she took the pants? What's she up to?"

"She wanted to get back at Jack for liking Cynthia."

"Maybe. But it's an awfully lame way to do it. I think she wants something else. You guys go to bed. I'll work on it."

The next morning, Katie was already up and eating her cereal by the time Jack and Josh came downstairs. She signaled to them to sit down and gave the thumbs-up behind her mother's back.

"Oh, I'm so excited. Tonight's the big night," trilled Mrs. Lexington, pouring a big glass of orange juice for Jack. "I've been telling Abner how marvelous you are onstage, Jack. You really should think of making a career of it."

A huge smile spread across Jack's face. "I will, madam, I promise you I will."

"Glad to hear it, young man," said Mr.

Lexington, looking up from his morning paper. "Don't rush off right away. I found my old yearbook with pictures of *Georgie, Grab Your Musket*. Thought you might like to have a look at it."

"Uh, maybe later, Dad," said Josh quickly. "We've got a lot to do for the show tonight, you know."

As soon as they'd wolfed down their breakfast, the kids rushed out the door to head for the bus stop.

"But the bus hasn't come!" said their mother.

But they were already on their way.

"So what did you figure out?" asked Josh as soon as they were walking down the driveway.

"I figured out what Lizzie wants. It's what she's always wanted. She wants to be Juliet with Jack."

"Duh," said Josh. "How does that help us?"

"Well, she's got something we want, and we've got something she wants — a part in the school play. It's perfect, isn't it?"

"This cannot be!" exclaimed Jack. "Why, 'tis bribery! And what of fair Cynthia? She was born to be Juliet, and I to be her Romeo. For once at least, I shall see a real girl play Juliet — and she must be the right girl."

"Jack, sometimes we don't get everything we want. I'll get your hourglass back to you. Trust me." At that moment the bus pulled up.

The kids climbed on board, and as they sat down, they could hear Frank and Evan snickering as usual in the back seat. Lizzie was smiling smugly and didn't look surprised when Katie settled in right beside her. "Oh, it's Katie Lexington, the famous actress. May I have your autograph?"

"Shut up, Lizzie," said Katie. "I want Jack's clothes back."

"What?"

"Don't play stupid with me or I'll tell the principal that Evan and Frank were messing with the fuse box last night. I saw them running away."

"What do I care if those bozos get caught?" She reached into her backpack and began brushing her hair.

"You want to be in the play, right, Lizzie?"

"No. I don't want to be in the play, Katie. I

want to *star* in the play — like I always do. Or like I always did before Jack Bradford showed up."

"You know Juliet's lines, don't you?"

"Every. Single. One."

"Hmmm," said Katie, taking her time. "I'll tell you what. I'll convince Jack to replace Cynthia with you if you give me back Jack's jeans and shirt — and anything you might have happened to find in the pockets." She was trying to be casual.

"Like this?" said Lizzie. She showed Katie the tiny hourglass, which was hanging from a chain she wore around her neck. Katie couldn't help herself. She gasped to see it so close.

"I *thought* this was something important. It's very interesting, you know. It's not like any hourglass I've seen before. No matter which way you hold it, the sand only runs in one direction. Doesn't it make a pretty necklace?"

"Give it to me, Lizzie. And you can star in the play."

"I'll star in the play first. And then I'll give it to Jack. That's my deal."

"Deal," said Katie, holding out her hand. The girls shook just as the bus lurched to a stop in front of the school. Everyone clambered out, and Katie just managed to grab Jack before he got caught up in the crush of kids heading to class.

"She's got it, Jack! I saw it. And she'll give it to you tonight. It's all taken care of."

"But what of Cynthia? Will she be Juliet?" He had to shout to her over the heads of bustling fifth-graders.

Katie shook her head. "I'm sorry, really. But I'll tell her in class, okay?"

"Hurry up! Hurry up!" Miss Larchmont, a teacher's aide, was saying. Speechless, Jack allowed himself to be swept along with Josh down the hallway toward Mrs. Pitney's room.

Lizzie sailed into the classroom after all the other students were seated. She touched Jack on the arm as she passed him. "Maybe we should go over our lines together at recess?" She smiled at him, but he pulled away and pretended to look out the window.

"Mrs. Pitney, Mrs. Pitney," said Lizzie a few minutes later, raising her hand.

"Yes, Lizzie?"

"Ahem," Lizzie cleared her throat. "I just wanted to remind everyone that *Romeo and Juliet* is tonight — and guess who's playing Juliet!" She gave a little curtsy and giggled. Frank and Evan started to clap, as did a few of Lizzie's friends. Josh leaned over to Jack, "Man, I am so sorry for you."

But Jack didn't say anything. All morning long, he stared straight ahead with his arms crossed, barely picking up his pencil and absolutely refusing to answer questions. Josh had never seen him so angry.

At lunchtime, Jack hurried out of the room and rushed toward the cafeteria without waiting for Josh or even going to his locker. Immediately, he found Cynthia at a table by herself, her lunch unopened in front of her. Her face was red and blotchy. Clearly, she'd been crying.

"How could you?" she said, turning to look at him. "I thought you said I was perfect as Juliet.

I've had so much fun rehearsing this play. I've never had such a big part before, and my parents are coming — *and* my grandparents from Florida. What am I going to say — 'Oh, at the last minute, Romeo decided he wanted a different girl'?"

"Despair not, noble Cynthia. All is not lost. 'Twas not my decision, but still tonight you shall shine on the stage like the glorious star you are. Put your trust in me."

"Really?"

She looks even prettier with tears in her eyes, thought Jack. "Really! Dry your eyes, prepare your costume, and meet me at the theater tonight." Jack touched his hand to hers and sat with her quietly through the rest of lunch. He was waiting until recess.

On the playground, Lizzie was standing on the top of the slide with a whole crowd of kids clustered around the bottom. "*Romeo, oh, Romeo, wherefore art thou, Romeo!*" she was saying over and over again. "There he is! There he is!" she shrieked when she saw Jack, but Jack walked past. He had to find Evan and Frank.

They were kicking at rocks over on the blacktop by the basketball hoop. As Jack came up to them, they looked up and sneered.

"Fear not. I carry no weapon," Jack said as he approached. He took his hands out of his pockets and held them in the air.

Evan hit Frank on the arm. "I've been telling you this kid might be dangerous," he whispered.

"I know. That's why I don't want him messin' with my sister."

Jack stood a few feet away from the boys and looked them up and down. "Your sister weeps, do you know that?"

"Oh, brother. Just 'cause she can't be in some stupid play? Give me a break! What a crybaby!"

"'Tis not right that she be not Juliet. Lizzie has not earned the part."

"That's true, Frank," said Evan. "Lizzie ain't been to many rehearsals."

"Fellows. We must lay down our arms and make peace. Name your conditions."

"Whaddaya talkin' about?" said Frank. "I can never understand anything this kid says, can you, Evan?"

"I want Cynthia to be in the play tonight," said Jack. "And you must help make it happen. Can I speak more plain than that?"

"Yeah?" said Frank, leaning back against the brick wall of the school. "What's in it for us?"

Jack hesitated. He looked across the playground, where under a group of trees, Cynthia stood talking with her friends. Then he spoke. "I promise to you, Frank Lubka, that if you let Cynthia perform tonight, I shall never speak to her again. In faith, I shall never see her again — nor you."

"We could make you do that? Leave town and all?" Evan couldn't believe what he was hearing.

"Aye, if tonight you keep Lizzie from the theater. And you must also bring to me the hourglass she is wearing about her neck. If you accomplish this, then I will ne'er take your sister's hand in marriage."

"What? You were gonna *marry* her? You're only twelve years old!" Frank took a step toward Jack.

Jack paused for a moment, a wicked twinkle in his eye. "*Younger than she are happy wives made.*"

Frank and Evan gave each other horrified looks. Frank pulled Evan to the side and whispered with him for a minute. Then he turned back to Jack. "All right. We'll do what you say. I've had it up to here with Lizzie Markle, anyway. She keeps bossing us around. But you had better not ever, and I mean *ever*, come near my sister again after tonight. Or this school, either. You hear me?"

Jack smiled. "I promise. If you but bring me the hourglass, I shall, after the play, disappear like a dream at daybreak."

Evan shook his head at Frank. "Can't this kid ever speak English?"

10 CURTAIN CALL

Backstage was bustling with activity when the Lexingtons and Jack arrived for the evening performance. Girls were running around looking for their costumes, peeking through the curtain at the audience, and taking a last nervous look at their lines. Lizzie, her hair elaborately covered in bows, was yelling at Mr. Tufnell, "I can't find my costume anywhere! Where is the blue dress? You have to find it now!"

Mr. Tufnell turned toward Jack with a look of relief, "Oh, Jack, I'm so glad you're here. Is Lizzie playing Juliet? I'm so confused! Didn't we rehearse the play with Cynthia?"

Lizzie, her hand on the hourglass around her neck, glared at Jack, "Explain it to him, Jack."

"Ah, Mr. Tufnell, Lizzie will tonight surprise us all with her performance, I assure you." He smiled. "But now, we must assemble the cast. I have a few words I wish to say."

Josh came over, unrecognizable in his nurse's costume. "I'm sorry again you've got to act with Markle tonight. But, I gotta say, Cynthia is being an awfully good sport about it." Cynthia was standing by herself, in the wings. She was still wearing her school clothes, a large backpack slung over her shoulder. She was gazing at Jack.

Jack just nodded and turned to the girls now standing around him. He looked at their excited faces before he began to speak.

"Friends, tonight you have changed the course of my life. Soon I will return home, but I will never leave what I have discovered this past month — the magic and splendor of the theater. Always, when I step upon a stage, I shall think of you and all that you have given me. Though I may be far away, I will be close in spirit." And he turned to look at Cynthia.

"Thank you, Jack," she whispered. At that moment, behind her appeared her brother, Frank, and Evan Ferrante. They stood side by side in the shadows.

"Hey, is Markle here?" asked Frank. "There're some kids out there in the hall who, you know, want her autograph or something."

"Me? Really?" squealed Lizzie, rushing forward. "Can I go and see them, Jack? Please, please, please! I'll put my costume on as soon as I get back."

"Go! Go! You must honor your fans." Jack smiled and Katie, suddenly realizing that something was up, caught his eye. He winked at her. Lizzie rushed off, following Evan and Frank. The door to the hallway slammed shut and Jack instantly turned to Cynthia. "Away with you, into your robes. In just moments the play will begin."

"What did you do?" asked Katie. Her hair was piled up under a hat, a sword hung at her side, and she was dressed just like Jack in doublet and hose.

"I saved the play!" said Jack. "Have no fear, good friend, all has been resolved."

"And you've got the hourglass?" The opening music had begun. The lights in the auditorium had begun to dim.

"Not yet, not yet," said Jack, rushing to take his place in the wings. "But we must trust the power of my threat! If Evan and Frank do not appear before Romeo marries Juliet, you must search for them. Off with you!" And he pushed Katie onstage, where she drew her sword just as the curtain rose.

Metal struck metal as the opening sword fight between the Capulets and the Montagues began. Soon Jack was strolling onstage as the love-struck Romeo, and then Josh waddled out with Cynthia for their first scene together. As soon as he appeared, there were muffled giggles in the audience, and before long, people were laughing out loud. The more they laughed, the more Josh settled into the role. He said his lines in a higher and higher voice, patted his huge stomach, and shamelessly hammed it up.

"You done good!" said Katie, patting her brother on the back as he exited into the wings.

"It's kind of fun!" he answered, his eyes sparkling. "But look!"

Romeo and Juliet were meeting for the first time. Slowly they danced around each other, their hands barely touching.

"How'd he get rid of Lizzie?" whispered Josh to Katie.

"I don't know. He didn't tell me. But wait, I've got to go on!" She leaped onstage.

At the end of each scene, the applause was loud. Josh kept getting more and more laughs. And the audience was almost breathless when Jack and Cynthia were onstage. They glowed in their parts of the lovers who would be together only three days.

During a costume change, Jack grabbed Josh. "Friend, have you seen the stinklings?" Somehow Josh knew he meant Evan and Frank, and he shook his head. Jack rushed back onstage.

Just as the worst fight was breaking out between the Capulets and Montagues, Evan and Frank stumbled through the door from the hallway. Their faces were covered in scratches, their shirts were torn, and they were out of breath. "Where's Jack?" they asked.

"Shhh!" Josh answered and pointed.

Without hesitation, Evan and Frank strode onstage. Katie, wielding her sword, took one look at them and screamed, "Zounds!"

"Hey, put that thing down! You could hurt somebody!" shouted Evan. The audience laughed, and at that moment Evan and Frank stared out into the blackness and realized the audience could see them. They froze and stared blankly ahead. The cast looked at each other helplessly. Only Jack kept his head.

"Gentlemen, for shame! Forbid this bandying on Verona's streets! Later I will take your trinket." He wrapped an arm around each of them, pulling them offstage. Quickly he whispered to Josh, "Retrieve the hourglass. Now!" He ran back just as Katie began her final speech before dying.

"Give me the hourglass," said Josh to Evan and Frank.

"Yeah," answered Frank. "But we had to go to a lot of trouble to get it. We better not ever see that kid again."

"If you give me the hourglass, you won't," said Josh.

"All right," said Evan, and he handed the small golden timepiece to Josh. "But we're sittin' right here to make sure he leaves right after the show." Frank and Evan plopped down on a pile of old scenery.

As soon as Jack finished the scene, the curtain came down for intermission.

"Have you it?" asked Jack.

"Right here," said Josh.

Jack took the golden hourglass from him and held it up to the light. "Alack! The grains run out! There is almost no time left!" He turned to Josh. "Josh, quickly, there can be no intermission if I am to finish the play. Places! Places! Dim the lights!"

The audience, just going out for brownies and juice, saw the lights going down and the curtain going up and returned to their seats. The actors hurried onto the stage.

Katie, whose character Mercutio was now dead, sat down beside Frank and Evan in the wings to watch the rest of the play. "So what'd you do to her?" she asked during a lull in the action.

"Principal's office," said Evan. "She thought even he wanted her autograph."

"He'll open it at the end of the night before he leaves. He's got his briefcase on the desk. He always brings his briefcase home," said Frank, who had spent a lot of time with the principal. "By the way, you died pretty good out there," he added, a little shyly.

"Thanks," said Katie and turned her attention back to the stage. Romeo, who was about to leave Juliet, was saying good-bye to her. As Jack bid Cynthia farewell, Katie thought she heard a new feeling in his lines.

"*Oh, think'st thou we shall ever meet again?*" Cynthia was saying.

"*Adieu! Adieu!*" said Jack. He ran offstage and nearly bumped into Josh.

"Friends," he said, seeing them both. "I will be off anon. Let us say farewells now."

"Really?" said Katie.

"He's that scared of us!" said Evan to Frank, elbowing him in the stomach.

"You have been like my poor lost sister this past month," he said to Katie. "And you," to Josh, "the brother I never had. And your mother, my mother. Remember me to your parents. And if e'er you find yourself in London, my home shall be yours."

"Can we do that — I mean, visit you and all?" asked Josh.

"I know not, but I will wish for it."

"Me, too!" said Josh. He hurried onstage for his final scene where he discovers the seemingly dead Juliet.

Katie and Jack just smiled at each other.

"Well, I'll wish that you become Shakespeare's most famous player!" said Katie finally.

"May it be so." Jack took out the hourglass again and looked at it. "And now to the conclusion of our play."

Juliet lay onstage on a piece of styrofoam

painted to look like a burial slab. Jack entered, pulled from his pocket a vial of poison, and swallowed it. *"Thus with a kiss I die!"* he uttered. He kissed Cynthia and fell to the ground.

Now Juliet awoke from her pretend death, only to find Romeo dead beside her. *"Thy lips are warm!"* she whispered. *"O happy dagger, this is thy sheath; there rust, and let me die!"*

"What?!" shouted Frank, leaping to his feet beside Katie. "You mean they *die*? They can't die! That's not fair!"

"Shhh! It's what happens," said Katie.

"But it's too sad," said Frank.

A sniffle made Katie look down. Evan was wiping at his eyes. "I don't like this play. I hate sad stuff," he was muttering.

The audience burst into applause and shouts of "Bravo! Bravo!" Katie rushed out to take her curtain call with the rest of the cast. The audience was on its feet wildly clapping, Mr. Tufnell was blushing, and Jack and Cynthia were stepping forward to bow. "Hurray for Jack!" yelled Katie.

"Hurray for Jack!" yelled Josh. "Hurray for Jack!" yelled the audience. Then, just as Mr. Tufnell was handing Cynthia a huge bouquet of flowers, the backstage door slammed open: Lizzie Markle stormed onto the stage.

She was carrying an enormous broom, which she started swinging wildly at the cast.

"She stole my play!" she yelled, heading straight for Cynthia. "She stole my play!" She was just about to bring the broom down on Cynthia's head when Jack grabbed the handle. But Lizzie wouldn't let go. She twisted and turned, yanking him from side to side. Jack held on tight.

Josh was trying to push through the crowd onstage to help, and Katie was just coming up behind Lizzie for a surprise attack, when Jack suddenly let go of the broom and fell over backward behind the styrofoam slab. Katie and Josh rushed to his side. They saw him falling, falling . . . but he never hit the ground.

Later, some kids said they'd heard a sonic boom when Jack and Lizzie were fighting. And some people in the audience claimed they'd seen an enormous flash of blue light. But Josh and Katie saw Jack disappear. One moment he was there with his arms spread back to catch his fall, the next he wasn't. In the blink of an eye he was gone. Completely gone.

EPILOGUE: ENCORE

After the show, parents and friends crowded backstage. Kids kept coming up to Josh and slapping him on the back, saying, "Man, you were so funny! I had no idea you were such a funny kid!" He signed a few programs. Cynthia's arms were full of flowers, and Mr. Tufnell was talking with her parents about sending her to drama camp next summer. Lizzie had eventually been subdued and sent home with her confused parents. "But, darling, I thought you had the lead, and you only had that little part at the very end," her mother kept saying.

Only Mr. and Mrs. Lexington noticed that Jack wasn't there. "Where's Jack?" said Mr. Lexington, looking around. "I wanted to tell him what a fine job he did out there. I particularly liked that last scene where he came back to life and battled that girl with the broom."

"Dad, that wasn't supposed to be in the play!" groaned Katie.

"I just want to find him and give him a hug!" said Mrs. Lexington.

"He had to go back, Mom. All of a sudden-like."

"Oh, that's just awful," fretted Mrs. Lexington. "I didn't even get to say good-bye to him!"

A few days later Mrs. Lexington was checking her e-mail and discovered one, surprisingly, from Jack.

"Noble Sir, Gracious Madam, I cannot thanke ye enough for opening thine home to me this month past. Your kindness has warmed my heart and given my life new possibilities. I have arrived home to discover that I have been granted a place at Shakespeare's Globe, and our first play is to be *Romeo and Juliet*. But I am to play the lady and not the gentleman! May God bless you and keep you well — all the rest of your days. Your devoted sonne, Jack."

"Oh, he called himself our son. How sweet," said Mrs. Lexington.

"Got home awfully fast, didn't he?" said Mr. Lexington. "Plane travel is something, isn't it?"

"I'm gonna miss him," said Josh.

"Me, too," said Katie. "I'll miss not having another brother around."

"Not for long," said Mrs. Lexington brightly. "There's also an e-mail here from Mr. Dee. He says our next guest will be here before we know it!"

BACK WITH JACK

London in 1599

You have the whole afternoon to yourself. What will you do? You might go down to the Thames River and watch the ships returning with treasures from the New World. Or you could decide to go to the bearbaiting (like a bullfight, but with an enraged bear) or go check out a new play at the Globe Theatre. Or maybe you'll go look at the cut-off heads of traitors rotting on London Bridge. Without television, movies, computer games, magazines, or even many books, watching the local executions is a favorite pastime.

While you are walking down the street, someone dumps a chamber pot from an upstairs window onto your head. That's the sewer system — the

street. You could go home and change your clothes — if you owned an extra set, which you don't. You could risk a cold bath on a cold day, but you don't. You wouldn't want to get a sore throat or a cough. Because you don't have antibiotics or very good indoor heating, you could die of strep throat or bronchitis. So you wipe off your face and keep on walking. Elizabeth I, the red-haired queen, has ruled your country for more than forty years, and she's made England rich and peaceful, but it's still a *very* rough place to grow up.

What Jack Wore

Your clothes are tight, itchy, and heavy. Mostly they are made of wool (England has a lot of sheep). Only very rich people wear silks and satins. On your legs you wear hose that are a lot like modern tights, except that they are much less elastic and they tend to bunch around your ankles. Over these you might wear "trunk hose," which look like puffy shorts, and a doublet or jacket.

If you are a girl, you wear a kirtle (a long dress). Nobody wears underwear — except for a long-sleeved, pullover linen shirt. By the way, this is usually the only piece of clothing you ever bother to wash!

Washing Up (or Not)

You wear a lot of perfume (if you can afford it) and carry a perfumed handkerchief to cover your nose. To take a bath, you have to carry water from a well or river to a tub, heat  the tub over a fire, and then get in it. That's a lot of work. Besides, you have to take off all your clothes in a really cold room. Why bother?

There are no official bathrooms. Instead, you keep a chamber pot under your bed or you might have a privy (a hole in the ground) in the backyard. Some people just use the fireplace or a convenient corner — even at the palace. Toilet paper has not been invented. Toothbrushes won't be invented for another fifty years, and don't even ask about deodorant. Fleas, lice, and bedbugs are common problems — even for the Queen.

Eating with Jack

You eat three meals a day of bread and beer. Sometimes you add beef or beans or eggs. For breakfast you might have a sop, a piece of bread soaked in red wine. Even the children drink beer or wine — there was no legal drinking age like we have today. Water is considered a dangerous drink, as it's often polluted (remember, no sewage system). Tea is unknown to you and will not become the nation's most popular drink for at least two hundred years.

Going to School

A large number of people do not know how to read and write. *Really*. If you do, you've probably been to a petty school where you learned the basics — reading, writing, and a little math. The alphabet you learn has only twenty-four letters —

i and *j* are considered the same letter, as are *u* and *v*. Most of the students are boys and are done with school by the time they are seven years old! Then they are off to work with their fathers or to be apprentices.

If your family has a little money, you go to grammar school, where you study Greek and Latin. If you are very fortunate, you might go on to a university. Shakespeare, the son of a glove maker, only went to grammar school. Still, he became the greatest writer in the English language.

But you won't be taught to spell. The first English dictionary won't be published for four more years, and like many people, you enjoy showing off how creative you can be with your spelling.

Getting Sick

Watch out! You can get smallpox, malaria, dysentery, measles, and of course, the bubonic plague — to name only a few. The plague, or Black

Death, is spread by the fleas on the rats that are everywhere in the crowded cities. Only you don't know that. And you don't have any antibiotics to cure you, anyway.

People do have herbal remedies, but your life expectancy in Elizabethan England is only forty-eight years. If you've made it through childhood, you're lucky.

Talk Like an Elizabethan

Today	1599 England
How are you?	How art thou?
Wait!	Stay!
Little girl	Poppet
Okay	Very well; 'Tis done
Wow!	Zounds! (short for "God's Wounds!")
Excuse me	Pray pardon; By your leave
Hello	Good day; Good morrow
Yes	Aye
No	Nay
Maybe	Mayhap
Why	Wherefore

Shakespeare's Theater

For just a few pennies, you can sneak out of work one day and go see a play at the Globe Theatre. In 1599, it has just been built by Shakespeare himself for his group of actors, The Lord Chamberlain's Men. It is shaped like an octagon, with an open pit in the center and a stage that sticks out into it. You stand there on the ground (that's why you are called a groundling) to watch the play. Around and above you in the roofed galleries sit the rich people.

The only lighting comes from the sun, the costumes are the hand-me-down clothes of rich people, and all the girls' parts are played by boys. It will be almost 100 years before girls are allowed to be actors.

In the audience, you do not sit politely watching the great William Shakespeare's plays. You shout and talk. You throw rotten food at characters you don't like. That's why the plays are filled with jokes and rough humor, sword fights, and terrible murders. Shakespeare wants to grab your attention!

A Summary of *Romeo and Juliet*

In Verona two noble families, the Montagues and the Capulets, are feuding.

Romeo Montague is upset about a girl who doesn't return his love. To cheer him up, his friends take him to a party—at Lord Capulet's house! At the party he meets and dances with the beautiful Juliet Capulet. Later that night, he comes to her balcony. They tell each other how much they love each other and decide to marry—the next day!

Juliet's old nurse and Romeo's friend, the Friar, help them marry in secret. Unfortunately, on the way home from his wedding, Romeo discovers his friend Mercutio fighting with Juliet's cousin Tybalt. When Mercutio is stabbed to death by Tybalt, Romeo kills Tybalt.

Romeo is banished. If he returns to Verona he will be killed.

Meanwhile Lord Capulet decides Juliet will marry Count Paris—the next day! Juliet doesn't know what to do. The Friar gives her a potion that will make it look like she is dead. Once she is in the family tomb, she will wake up and the Friar will take her to Romeo. But Romeo misses the message from the Friar and races to Juliet's tomb. Believing her dead, he takes poison. Moments later, Juliet awakens to find her Romeo dead beside her. She stabs herself.

At last, the families realize the terrible consequences of their hatred.

As with many of his plays, Shakespeare did not invent this story. It was already popular as a poem called "The Tragical History of Romeus and Juliet." But it was Shakespeare's amazing writing that has made it endure as a favorite for over 400 years.

ABOUT THE AUTHOR

Perdita Finn lives in the Catskill Mountains
with her husband, two children, four cats,
and an overweight dachshund.
If she could go back in time to Elizabethan
England, she'd love to see the first performance
of Shakespeare's play *The Winter's Tale*.
Can you figure out why?